Morty's Holiday

BRÝN GROVER

Copyright © 2026 Brýn's Quill

ISBN: 979-8-9908001-7-5

All rights reserved.

No part of this publication may be reproduced, distributed, or transmitted in any form or by any means, including photocopying, recording, or other electronic or mechanical methods, without the prior written permission of the publisher, except as permitted by U.S. copyright law. For permission requests, contact grover.author@gmail.com

The story, all names, characters, and incidents portrayed in this production are fictitious. No identification with actual persons (living or deceased), places, buildings, and products is intended or should be inferred.

Book Cover: A skeleton wearing a hat having a drink (vignette for the feast of the dead) by José Guadalupe Posada ca. 1892, Open Access File Source Image from Metropolitan Museum of Art

Edited and formatted by 360 Editing. (a division of Uncomfortably Dark Horror). Editor: Candace Nola

Contents

Dedication	V
1. Chapter One	1
2. Chapter Two	11
3. Chapter Three	18
4. Chapter Four	23
5. Chapter Five	29
6. Chapter Six	34
7. Chapter Seven	42
8. Chapter Eight	47
9. Chapter Nine	55
10. Chapter Ten	59
11. Chapter Eleven	63

12.	Chapter Twelve	69
13.	Chapter Thirteen	72
14.	Chapter Fourteen	77
15.	Chapter Fifteen	82
16.	Chapter Sixteen	89
About the Author		97

Dedication

For Tiffini who puts up with my jokes, provides inspiration, and took me on a cruise in the first place.

Chapter One

Stepping off the ramp of the cruise ship and taking a deep breath, Morty stopped and looked around him. He could not believe he was finally taking time for himself. He was getting a chance to unwind. Forget work. Bask in the moment. He leaned back and looked up at the palm trees waving in the wind above him and shouted. "Carpe diem!"

Use all your senses. He remembered hearing someone tell him that before he left for the cruise. Closing his eyes, he focused on the smell of the ocean as the breeze wafted the salty air past him. *That's so much better than the obnoxious smells of the city.*

Satisfied, he kept his eyes closed and tried to focus on sounds. Laughing. People talking. Seagulls chirping. Waves jostled around the ship behind him. *That's different too. No traffic horns. No cussing. No sirens.*

Taste would wait. He'd find himself a nice little place to sit down and try some of the local delicacies at his leisure. No rushing to finish a meal this week. It was all about unwinding. His mouth watered as he thought about eating.

Opening his eyes and turning around to look at the ship that was proving to be his salvation, he felt a hot spray hit his neck and side of his face. Something else hit him on his left calf, disturbing his moment of reflection.

Pulled away from his contemplation and examination of his senses, he looked to see what disrupted his concentration. A head was lying on the ground next to him. A body not far away. The laughter he had heard while exploring his senses had turned into terrified screaming. He looked back around to see people running in his direction. Someone grabbed his arm and started yelling at him.

"What the fuck are you doing? That was mine. I had the orders."

"What? What in tarnation are you talking about?" Morty was trying to decipher the chain of events unfolding around him.

"You don't belong here. But you come in swinging your scythe around. Now you've killed someone on my list. How the fuck am I supposed to meet my quota or fulfill this order if you're bogarting my pickups?"

"Wait, what? I'm just here on vacation. I'm not working at all."

"Dumbass, you just killed my mark."

"But I was just standing here enjoying the smells and sounds. I merely turned to look at the ship and sea one last time before heading off to explore and find someplace quiet to eat. I haven't stolen anyone's mark, yours or otherwise." Morty said, confused.

"Really dumbass? Well, when you turned around, you swung your scythe and cut off my mark's head. Don't deny it. The body is right next to you. The head is at your feet. The blood splatter is all over you."

"Holy shit. I didn't go after your mark. I swear. I'm just here on vacation. I don't even think about the scythe. It's just slung over my back. You know we can't leave them behind. It's like an appendage. But I'm not actively using it. I'm not here on business at all."

"Lot of good that does me. Now there will be reports to fill out." He paused as he looked at Morty. Sighing and taking a deep breath, he looked at the crowd gathering around the body. "HOW THE FUCK AM I SUPPOSED TO MEET MY QUOTA NOW! I'll be one behind on my assignments because of you. Why don't you stow that blade, idiot? You don't have to keep that thing fully open in reaper position. It folds up against the staff. Or has your vacation robbed you of your memory?"

"Sorry. This was not planned. But I am sure there is a protocol for weird scenarios. It will work out for your quota and reports. I'd be happy to be a witness and tell whomever you want that you were here for the job at hand and an accident occurred. I don't want credit." Morty replied quickly.

Paramedics and police seemed to arrive simultaneously and were ushering onlookers away from the body and cordoning off the scene. No one paid attention to Morty or his companion, even though they were standing close to the body.

Morty's scythe was not visible to normal human eyes. Other reapers could see it. Very old people and children could sometimes see it. There were those few who had what they called 'the sight' in this line of work who could see beyond the veil. Those closer to death and those who still believed in the magic of the world around them also had the ability to see it.

Very rarely an empath could either see or feel its presence. They somehow knew it was there, and that he was a reaper but couldn't place their fingers on it. Sometimes, it was just a gut feeling that they knew. But no one ever believed anyone when they pointed it out. Human blood on his clothes also became invisible to humans.

Neither the paramedics nor the police noticed anything out of place with him or his companion. They were just two more people standing near a newly decapitated body.

Their presence meant little in the throng of people coming and going from the cruise ship. They were not covered in blood. No one was pointing at them or calling them out for potentially being involved. They were just there among a throng of other people. Authorities were trying to calm some of the witnesses while also trying to make sense of what happened.

They drew no attention from anyone near the scene except Gary and Katie as they exited the ship. Ignoring them much as the others were doing, the couple walked down the pier towards the meeting point for their excursion that day.

"What do you think all that commotion was about?" Katie asked as they continued walking.

"Looks like a task order was being fulfilled. Nothing with which to concern ourselves." Came the reply.

"Oh. You told me we were taking a trip. I swear to God, Gary, if you are working that's the final straw for me."

"Nothing like that, babe. I didn't know this was happening. We are on vacation, and no one is to even call me. So, let's go about our day and enjoy it. Forget this situation on the pier. It's not our problem."

"Ok. But you better be telling the truth."

While the crowd behind them seemed to grow even larger, trying to see what was going on or get a view of the newly decapitated man, Morty and his companion stepped backwards 10 feet more than they had already.

"Just claim the pickup in your report." Morty said. "I'm not taking credit for it. Like I said, I'm just trying to take a vacation."

"You know I can't. They track everything. You've screwed me today. It's not like there is a makeup list of pickups to fill things out. I'll be short one this week. Thanks, a lot, dumbass."

"Sorry, if there is anything I can do to help make it right, I will."

"It might help. WTF? Try watching what the fuck you are doing while you're down here. And for fuck's sake, stow the blade, dumbass. If you are truly on vacation, you don't need it out."

This vacation is not off to a good start.

"Yeah. Sure. I got excited about getting away for a little while. I'm just tired of killing all the time. As you know, the quotas are a bitch. Task orders never stop coming, especially with city duty; it never fuckin' ends. I imagine it is more peaceful on the islands or out in the country."

"Whatever. I don't give a fuck about your issues. I have a job to do. Just stay clear of my assignments."

Walking away shaking his head, Morty looked up and down the shoreline trying to find a nice quiet place to relax, away from people, and where he couldn't accidentally decapitate anyone. Of course, he would rectify that when he stowed the blade into a folded travel position. Fortunately for him, most of the cruise line guests signed up for specific excursions or planned on hitting up the bars. The beaches themselves were mostly empty. He'd be safe from anything happening to him or anyone else and have the whole day before having to get back on the ship later in the afternoon.

With a determined step, he headed off the pavement and onto the sand. A small stand of trees about 100m away looked like the perfect spot. Shade and isolation from people.

I guess the good thing about a horrible start to a vacation is that it can only get better from here.

After settling into a beach chair, Morty quickly fell asleep and dreamed about how he could really dive into that last sense. Taste. He was going to take full advantage of this vacation. He knew it wouldn't be long before he was back to work.

He was visibly smiling even though he was dozing. He could almost taste the spicy flavors as he fantasized about slowly enjoying a meal and embracing the flavors of the island. He even started drooling a little bit in his sleep.

Awakened by the wet feeling of his own spittle on his chin, Morty reached up to wipe it off with the sleeve of his cloak.

As he did, a young couple was running and skipping across the sand, holding hands and laughing. They were enjoying each other's company in the bliss of a sunny day at the beach. At least for a while. When they were passing Morty, the girl looked at him and stopped in her tracks and pointed at him.

"What the hell happened to him?" She asked. "He's covered in blood and sitting there with a scythe on the beach."

"What are you talking about?" Her boyfriend asked. "That dude? He's just chilling and enjoying the day."

"But the blood. It's all over."

"What blood? Are you alright?"

Hearing this conversation, Morty knew she knew that he was a reaper. Or at least she saw things others didn't see.

She's not a reaper or old. Perhaps an advanced empath. Maybe she was born with the sight. Be calm. Don't react to her in a way that would attract attention.

Feeling uneasy, he waved at the couple. He managed a sheepish smile.

Seeing his friendliness, the boyfriend smiled and walked towards him.

"He's harmless. Let's just say hi and move on and enjoy our day."

"NO!" She screamed it out. "You don't understand. He's a killer. Something's off. He's way too dangerous. I can feel it. I can see it."

"Honey, we took this trip to relax. I'm looking right at him. Everything is okay."

As the man walked towards Morty with his hand outstretched, Morty stood. When he did, he was startled as an unusually large Doberman darted out of the trees, passed him, and leaped onto the man. Tearing at his throat and attacking him with such violence that the man didn't have a chance to scream.

The girl ran away screaming and pointing at the scene behind her. Drawing the attention of the few others up and down the beach as well as people from the nearby boardwalk, she continued moving away, terrified of both the man and the dog.

Morty went to try to pull the dog off the man but was unable to control the animal's rage and strength. He struggled with all his might to get this dog off the man. It was enraged and in the throes of trying to kill him, if it hadn't already done so.

After a short period of struggle, the dog finally loosened his grip and slowly backed away from its victim. Its eyes were focused on the downed man for any sign of movement. Heavy breathing and growling emitted from its massive chest as blood dripped from its jaw.

Security guards came running down the beach. With all the shouting and people running, the Doberman took off as if it were being chased by something larger and more dangerous.

Behind the security guards, a reaper rushed to the scene. He stood and watched the situation intensely.

Checking the pulse, the guards determined the man was likely dead. But one began CPR while the other radioed in for an ambulance and paramedic support.

"He better not die, you motherfucker."

Morty looked at the newest arrival on the scene.

"Huh? Well, hopefully not. That dog just attacked, but I don't know how much damage was done."

"If he dies, I'll have your ass."

"What the fuck are you talking about? I was minding my own business as they walked by. I waved, and he reached out his hand to say hello when that beast attacked him." He said as he pointed to where the dog had been only to see it had taken off like a bat out of hell.

"Bull shit. That was my mark, and you took him too early. You stirred that dog up and drove it into a rage so that it attacked him. I already had things set up farther down the beach for them to fall into a hole filled with spiked poles that some kids put into the sand as part of a 'pretend we're guerilla fighters' game."

As he said that, a fresh onset of screaming could be heard farther down the beach. The woman had come across the pit of spiked poles and impaled herself to death right in front a family who was having a picnic nearby. They were screaming at the scene in front of them.

"You fucked up my plans and my headcount, asshole." He said to Morty as he looked down the beach towards where the woman had just impaled herself.

Shaking his head, Morty informed him that he did nothing. He wasn't responsible for the dog, the timing, or anything.

As the ambulance arrived and parked as close as possible, the paramedics came and took over the situation with the dog victim. One security guard took off running down the beach to respond to the other incident while one remained behind to take reports. Morty was asked a few questions but allowed to go free.

Maybe I should just go back to my cabin and sit out on the deck with my feet up. Enjoy the sun and breeze from there. I can always order food for delivery from my butler & concierge team. This is too much today.

Chapter Two

When his cell phone rang, Jim noticed the caller ID was his boss. *WTF now?* He hesitated but answered on the 4th ring. No sense in pissing off the man.

"Hey boss. Wasn't expecting you. Everything ok?" He asked, knowing it wasn't. The boss never called him about anything good. More work. Complaints about work. Cutbacks. More quotas. There was never a good call. Never a *'how you doin'?'* welfare check.

"Jim, I don't know how you managed to do it. But getting Morty to reap while he's on vacation is pretty amazing. That's a half-time speech we're going to need to recreate for all supervisors to use. I'll admit I was skeptical about the whole vacation thing. But getting one done early in the morning while on vacation isn't bad. Hell, it's damn near legendary!"

Jim was dumbfounded. He had no idea what his boss was talking about. Morty was on a cruise, but he didn't have any assignments. He was vociferous about not doing any reaping at all. He was burned out and threatened to quit fulfilling any task orders if he didn't have a break. And that would be problematic for Jim, his boss, and the whole division. Disciplinary actions aside, training and getting a new reaper up to speed could not be done in short order. The training and apprenticeship took time. Recruiting alone seemed to take longer and longer these days.

"What are you talking about, Joe? He's on vacation. Like a real human vacation, away from work with no jobs to do."

"Well, the numbers came in this morning, and the bean counters let me know. Whatever you said to him is working. Keep up the good work." He said as he ended the call.

Hurry back. We need you. That's the only thing Jim could remember saying to Morty after begrudgingly approving his vacation request and informing other team members and bosses. Hardly a pep talk, much less some "*Win one for the Gipper*" kind of moment. Knute Rockne he was not.

Gary and Katie returned to the cruise ship after a full day out, which included a gastro tour of the island's cuisine. Bloated and tired, they walked slowly. Burping and farting to Katie's disapproval, Gary worked his way forward slowly. He moved so sluggishly they almost missed the ship.

"For God's sake, control yourself, Gary. We were almost late."

"But we're on the elevator, aren't we? No harm, no foul." Belching again, he laughed.

"No harm maybe. No foul? Well, I'd argue that with the noxious fumes coming out of you. You're a disgusting slob."

"But you married me. Willingly at that!"

When they got to their room, Gary noticed he'd missed three calls. When he heard Katie moaning, he put the phone down. *They can wait. I gave them orders not to bother me this week.*

Morty was getting noticed while trying to disappear and relax. He hoped the afternoon in his cabin would be uneventful. After showering off sand and changing clothes, he ordered room service. The good thing about this cruise line is that they tried to adjust the menus to match the local cuisines for anyone who didn't want to get off the ship. He could order a Mango Jerk Chicken and engage in the fifth sense in peace and solitude on his deck.

When his cabin doorbell rang, Morty smiled and got up to answer it. The thought of the Mango Jerk Chicken fusion had his mouth watering. Waiting at the door in his crisp suit with a white napkin neatly folded and lying over the arm which was skillfully holding the silver-domed tray of food stood his assigned butler.

Since he was in a higher-cost cabin, it came with butler service. And this guy took servicing his clients very seriously. He stood there smiling even though the suit and the hot tray of food conspired to form beads of sweat on his freshly shaven bald head. He did not complain. He merely smiled and greeted Morty.

"Here's your order, sir." He said as he did a half bow flourish of sorts without any movement of the food tray whatsoever. "Where would you like me to put it?"

"Oh, on the kitchen table is fine. I'm just sitting on the deck chilling, anyway. I can stay in the room to eat." Morty replied, smiling and nearly slobbering with the anticipation of piling the food into his mouth.

"Oh no, we can't have that. There is a table on the deck. I will take it out there and get it set up for you properly. That way, you can continue to enjoy the sea breeze and views while you eat. It's no trouble at all."

"Oh, that's nice of you. Thank you." Morty smiled but was a little annoyed as well since he now felt like he had to add an extra cash tip on top of the prepaid tips he'd applied to this cruise.

He fished around in his pants looking for some money to give the butler. Finding none, he started towards his bedroom to grab something. As he rummaged through his nightstand looking for tip money, he heard some commotion coming from the balcony.

A seagull with a fresh queen conch had dropped it right on the butler's head to break it open and get at the delicacies inside. The bird may have thought the bald head was a rock he could use to break open the prize. Being about four pounds in size, it hit the butler with deadly force as the gull dropped it from a height of maybe seven meters.

Concussed and likely sporting a skull fracture, the butler dropped the tray, which made the noises that Morty heard from the bedroom. Mango jerk chicken and sides splattered on the deck.

Disoriented, grabbing his head and stumbling, the butler leaned too far over the railing on the balcony, and fell into the water. Morty ran to the deck but did not see the butler hit the sea. It happened so fast, he was already underwater and out of view from that angle.

The cries of people on lower decks who saw him fall led to a quick rescue effort by nearby fishing boats and others sailing in the calm waters where the cruise ship was docked. Several of them converged in the area at the same time.

Morty was flabbergasted. *Not again. What the fuck is going on?* Leaving the cabin in a hurry, he ran to the elevator and went down to the gangway, hoping to find a way around the ship from the docked side to the sea-facing side of the ship. But there wasn't one.

Rescuers coming from different directions nearby seemed to converge on the area quickly. The butler was found underwater and pulled out quickly. He was not breathing. Once put onto a boat, CPR started on him as the boat moved to get him to the docks for proper care. An ambulance had already been called and was on the way.

Morty stood dumbfounded and worried as he tried to find out what was happening. Then the boat with the butler pulled up in front of the ship just as an ambulance could be seen heading to it. He ran from the back end of the ship where he had been standing and got to the location after the ambulance arrived and paramedics were working on the butler.

But it was too late. The butler had died from the fall or from the brain injury of the clam hitting his skull. Neither the crew of the fishing boat nor the paramedics could revive him. As a sheet was pulled over his head and the body loaded into the ambulance for transport and care, Morty trudged his way through the crowds and back to his cabin.

Things were not going well. But he was still hungry and wanted to taste that mango jerk chicken. Entering, he looked to see the mess on his balcony. His food was all over the deck. And near the silver dome that once sat upon the tray lay a cracked clam that a couple of seagulls were fighting over.

He shuffled towards the deck, and the birds flew away at his sudden entrance into their food fight. *Fuckin' A. I'll have to reorder the food, and who knows how long it will take now with a dead butler.*

With all the commotion, the kitchen told him they could not deliver any food for hours and suggested that Morty go to one of the many restaurants and bars on the cruise ship to get something to eat. Apologizing for the inconvenience, they abruptly hung up. Morty was pissed. Hangry, as they say. The butler's accident notwithstanding, he was not the one who did the cooking. Surely the kitchen itself could continue to function, and someone else could deliver room service.

With this crap news, Morty decided to head up to the Lido deck. He knew they had a couple of bars where food was served. And he could relax in the setting sun and enjoy whatever entertainment was taking place there.

Chapter Three

When he arrived, the place was starting to fill up. The pools were already full. But seats and lounge chairs near the stage and around the few bars on the Lido deck were filling up fast. He managed to find one that was within view of the stage but also close enough to a bar that he could be waited on easily.

Grabbing the attention of one of the servers, he got a menu and ordered a daiquiri. As the waiter walked away, he perused the menu. *No Mango Jerk Chicken. Fuckin' figures. Fuckity fuck fuck. This is all just pub food crap. Not at all the taste extravaganza I envisioned today. So much for indulging in all five senses.*

When the waiter returned, Morty reluctantly ordered the fish and chips.

"Very well, sir. It should be out before the show starts."

"What's the entertainment tonight?"

"Oh, some sort of acrobatic show set to lights and music. I saw part of the earlier one. It's pretty good. And the athleticism of the team is downright amazing."

"Thanks." Morty replied as the waiter moved off to place his order.

While waiting for the food, he sipped his daiquiri. Then he thought about using it for his taste experience. Closing his eyes, he took another sip. He focused on the flavor. *It's kind of silky. There's a kind of citrusy tang to it. The sweetness mixes well with the lime and rum to create a crisp flavor from the syrupy concoction. This is nice. Not Mango Jerk Chicken. But nice.*

Holding the glass under his nose to fully utilize the sense of taste in conjunction with smell, he noticed in his next sip there was a creamy and vanilla-like flavor as well. *Very nice.*

Satisfied that he had finally experienced the sense of taste, he sat back to relax and enjoy the upcoming show. This was way better than the rest of the trip had been up to this point.

His fish and chips were brought out just as the light show began for the entertainment. The show started off with some high-flying trapeze acts while a couple engaged in Tissu acrobatics, clinging to long pieces of fabric and seemingly contorting their bodies into motions that were fluid and mesmerizing. Their various drops and slides made it hard to focus on the trapeze stuff. It was a sensory overload of entertainment.

As the show continued, the dancers moved about like seamless parts of one overall body. The music blared with a deep and resonating bass. Lights flickered as spotlights moved around, highlighting different parts of the stage.

This is a good show for the senses. Sights and sounds rolled into one wonderful experience.

Morty gasped when one of the men in the group started juggling in his Rola Bola act. He was intrigued by the way the man could balance himself on a board on a cylinder while rolling left and right and still successfully juggling.

Amazing talent and body control.

Fire acts happened while a unicycle rider crossed the stage doing additional juggling. There was so much going on it wasn't possible to take it all in at the same time. The show had something for everyone. You could focus on the acts you liked, and the others would be background motions.

On the other side of the deck, Gary and Katie watched the same show.

"Wow, there's a lot going on here."

"Sure is." Katie agreed. "What do you want to do tomorrow?"

"Ha! I know you want to look for stones. Nice try."

Smiling, she nodded. "Good boy."

"I'm game. That's part of the reason we went on this cruise. Other than getting away from my never-ending responsibilities, we wanted to look for hag stones and other things for the oddities shop and shows for you."

"Yes! My turn tomorrow. As long as my stomach holds up. That pain comes and goes. But it was pretty sharp last night."

"I remember. You whimpered a lot in your sleep too."

"Sorry. I'm feeling pretty good right now. Just some pressure and discomfort in the abdomen. The feeling of urgency to go to the bathroom comes and goes. But no pain to speak of or nothing more than a 1 if I had to rate it from one to ten."

"Good. I'm glad to hear that the pain is down. But we do need to get this checked when we get home, just to be on the safe side. Meanwhile, let's plan on the stones tomorrow, and then if we have to call an audible in the morning, we can. Your health and comfort are more important."

Katie smiled and tenderly touched his shoulder. "Thank you, honey."

When the stage cleared, the whole troupe came out to bow to the audience as one and revel in the cheers of the crowd for a job well done. It was their last show of the evening, and they were happy to have had a great show and to be done for the day.

"It's over. Let's go back to the room before the encore and beat the crowds to the elevator." Gary said.

"Good idea. And then stones tomorrow!" She giggled.

As the performers started to disperse, many did somersaults as they were exiting the stage. One person bumped into another as they were both doing it. One was flipping forward and one was flipping backward. The backflipping performer hit the other performer in the face with his feet and knocked him over.

Falling off the stage, he landed hard on his back before bouncing to the ground.

The screaming started immediately. Performers rushed to the fallen acrobats from all directions.

Morty watched the scene unfold. Remembering his other terrible experiences of the day, he shook his head in disbelief. *Not again.*

"Why can't I just have peace and quiet?"

As performers rushed forward and crowded around their injured associate, the body language became obvious. The spinal cord injury was fatal. The tragic accident had broken his back.

Morty had already signed his check, charging the meal to his room, before the show had ended. So, he quietly got up and started to make his way back to his cabin as the ship crew continued to rush past him.

Chapter Four

The phone was ringing off the hook while Jim was in the shower. He would have ignored it altogether. But it was his boss. He knew because he'd paid for one of those specialty ringtones. Whenever his boss called, the phone played *'asshole line 1, asshole line 1'*. So, he jumped out of the shower and wrapped a towel around himself as quickly as he could on his way into the master bedroom to pick up his cell phone. Even though he had not bothered to rinse or dry off, his haste was insufficient. The phone stopped ringing before he got there.

In a state of panic, he picked it up to redial. He knew the boss was a stickler for immediately answering calls. It did not matter whether it was during normal business hours or not.

This wasn't a typical 9-to-5 job. Sure, he technically had those kinds of hours, but they were mostly for paperwork and calls. The business of death is a twenty-four hour a day one. There were expectations. The pay reflected these inconveniences.

Redial hit. Joe answered on the first ring.

"Where the fuck were you?"

"Hi boss." *Not even a greeting. Just straight to yelling.* "I was in the shower and couldn't get to the phone in time." Jim explained.

"Take the phone with you into the bathroom from here on out. I shouldn't have to wait until it stops ringing and then wait some more for you to call me back."

"Yes, sir." *Fucking prick*. "What's up?"

"We have an accounting issue right now. I need you to get in touch with Morty and figure out what's going on so we can straighten this out."

"Accounting issue?"

"Did I stutter, dumbass?"

The pause after that question made Joe think he actually wanted a response instead of being the rambling rhetorical question of a megalomaniac. "No..." Jim was cut off before he finished the first word.

"Shut up. I don't need you to answer. It appears that a lady scheduled to be picked up with her husband in a particularly gruesome accident on a beach died after the husband was attacked by a dog. Both deaths were assigned reapings. But Morty went and grabbed the man without authorization and beat the assignee to the punch. But the girl is a problem. No one knows who it belongs to now. Since it was supposed to be a two for one reaping, and ended up being two separate reapings, they are up in arms in accounting. Adherence to task orders are important. They take them seriously. Deviations and modifications of contracts create problems."

Joe paused while he took a drink of bourbon. Jim was smart enough to know the boss hadn't really stopped talking. Keeping his mouth shut was the way to go. Like a kid growing up, he knew there were circumstances where 'speak only when spoken to' took on additional nuances. Working for Joe was one of those circumstances.

"Accounting does not want to award two kills since it was supposed to be a package deal. So, the options are to figure out if Morty gets credit for both or neither. Unfortunately, he was already given credit for the man in the preliminary review. So, if he gets neither, there's a lot of nasty and time-consuming paperwork involved, and will result in a separate inquest. Do I make myself clear?"

Jim wasn't sure. He thought he knew the direction the boss was going. This wasn't a 'find out what happened' kind of assignment. This was a 'find a way to fix the narrative and keep accounting happy' kind of mission.

"Yes, sir. I'm sure Morty should get credit for both kills and allow accounting to mark it down as the two for one reaping, which was already sanctioned."

"Good. Make it happen fast. The vultures are circling, and upper management is being hounded by accounting, all while passing the buck on to me. And this shit is going to roll down on you fast if you don't get it straightened out. We're just lucky they haven't been able to get in touch with the new director for this hemisphere. We need to get it fixed before they reach him or before he's back from vacation. New bosses like to reorganize and fire people to show their power and make it look good on paper. Morty is out there providing targets for the inevitable layoffs."

Joe hung up the phone before Jim could acknowledge anything further. *What an asshole.*

I wish he was someone's next assignment.

When Jim got Morty on the phone, the conversation was mostly one-sided. Shit did roll downhill, and now it was a festering pile of dung heading straight to Morty.

"Look, you're on vacation. But you're making kills. On the one hand, everyone is amazed and happy, impressed even. On the other hand, you are creating accounting nightmares up and down the chain. Someone is going to pay for this, and it ain't going to be me."

"What do you mean?"

"The dog attack kill was assigned to you."

"How is that possible? I had nothing to do with it. I tried to save the guy from the dog. For real, boss, I didn't do it."

"Immaterial. You got the kill. The other team is properly pissed off. But accounting made the call, and that's the way it is. But the girl was supposed to be part of a double job."

"I did not touch her or go near her." Morty defended himself. "She ran down the beach and met her demise. Even with the pre-planned accident, it isn't my fault or my kill. That trap was already set for her, and she died in it. That went according to plan."

"Bullshit. That's where we have a serious problem. Accounting cut the order for a two for one reaping. The time lag between the two deaths is the biggest problem. They were supposed to die together. You screwed that up. You can't get credit for one and the other guy credit for one. They'd have to have two entries for a single-entry task order. Not only will accounting refuse to accept that arrangement, but Joe won't either–not to mention his boss. No one knows how he'd react to such a screwed-up situation. Thankfully, accounting hasn't reached him yet."

"But that's what happened. I didn't really have anything to do with the guy, for that matter."

"I hear you. And it remains immaterial. That kill is yours. So, the girl must be yours as well."

"How? That doesn't make sense."

"It doesn't need to be perfect, Morty. Here's the story we are going to tell, and if it comes to an inquest of any kind, we have to stick to the story or multiple heads will roll—including mine and yours."

"I see. What's the story?"

"While you accidentally killed the man, for which you've already received credit, you also accidentally killed the girl out of the planned timeline."

"How do we back that up?"

"Fear. We have to play it up to fear. When the man was killed, she was afraid. She ran down the beach screaming. Is that not so?"

"Yes. That part is true."

"Good. It's important to have some truth in there that can be verified in order to back up our story...your story. She ran in fear, and as a result, she fell into the pit with spikes and was killed."

"That's also true, even though I didn't do anything."

"But you did, Morty. You did. Pay fucking attention here. You. Scared. Her. You used your powers and her ability to see the blood on you to drive her into a straight-up run of terror to her own demise. And since it happened earlier than the scheduled dual reaping of the couple, it counts as your kill. You killed them both. That's that. That's what we're telling Joe and what we're telling accounting. That's what's going to be recorded in the logbooks. That's what's going up the chain of command."

Reluctantly, Morty agreed.

"The funny thing about this is you are in a position to potentially get a commendation for your work while on vacation. I know you say you are not working. But keep up the good work, anyway."

"Um, well, I really just want to chill from the chase and the kill."

"Chill away. It is working in our favor, anyway."

With that, Jim hung up. Morty put down his cell phone and went to the balcony of his suite on the cruise ship. Looking out over the sea, he shook his head in disbelief. Then he started thinking about the next port of call and how he could just disappear and be alone to relax and unwind.

Chapter Five

When the cruise ship docked at the luxury liner's private island of Fargo Cay, Morty was ready to disembark and get away from everyone. Just to make sure he had no mishaps, he waited a couple of hours for everyone else leaving for beach time or other excursions to depart the ship. While he waited anxiously, he sat on his deck and looked out over the calm Caribbean Sea and lit up a cigar. In all the commotion and excitement, he had forgotten he had a box of premium Cuban cigars.

He took his time and focused on his previous mantra of enjoying the senses. It was nice to enjoy a smoke without the chemical smell that came with cheaper cigars. Closing his eyes as he rolled the smoke around in his mouth and exhaled, he focused on the richness of the flavor with both his tongue and his nostrils. *Earthy. Woody. Authentic. Even a floral touch of some sort I can't quite make out.*

As time moved forward, he neared the end of his cigar. Relishing the finishing smell and taste that would linger for a few minutes even after he was done, he took his last puff and put the cigar out. It was time to leave the ship and get some much-needed R&R.

IN ANOTHER CABIN, GARY asked Katie how she was feeling.

"Minimal pain. Nothing that will stop me. Let me go to the bathroom before we head out. For some reason I can't stop peeing. It's almost like I'm 9 months pregnant and a baby is lying on top of and kicking my bladder at the same time."

"Don't even joke about pregnancy. The last thing we need at our age is to start over again with a baby."

"If I was pregnant, the doctor's got a lot of explaining to do about that vasectomy."

"Or YOU have a lot of explaining to do!"

"Shut up, asshole. I'll be ready in a minute, and we can head out to look for some hag stones and anything else that will be good for my shop."

"Yes, ma'am!" Gary said jokingly.

When Morty got to the beach of Fargo Cay, he took a moment to enjoy the breeze and sounds of the ocean. He stood still for a moment, looking up and down the beach. Spotting a location that was void of people, he headed in that direction. He didn't even bother to get a chair rental or bring a towel with him from the ship.

He just walked until he could barely see anyone in the distance and lay down on the ground. Watching the clouds and daydreaming, he remained still. *Now this is the life. Finally, some peace and quiet.* Hours passed in blissful repose.

Going a different way around the Cay, the couple searched for the prized stones. Being a small island, it wasn't long before they wound almost the entire way around it with limited success until they found a rock-strewn section of beach which was around the bend and out of sight from where Morty lay relaxing.

Katie and Gary walked slowly and carefully among the rocks looking for hag stones. They tended to sell well in her curiosity shop back home. They had only found one prior to getting to this rocky section of shore, but they were not there long when Katie indicated it was time to leave and head back to the ship. Gary stalled and kept looking.

"I have to pee."

Looking at her with disdain, considering their relative lack of success in finding enough hag stones to make up for the effort, he shook his head disparagingly.

"Can't you hold it? It's not time to board yet. We should try to find more stones or other items of interest for your shop in order to add more value to the outing."

"No, I've been holding it. We need to get back to the ship. I told you before; I can't seem to stop peeing. Now I'm about ready to burst."

"Just squat down over there behind the boulder."

"What the fuck is wrong with you? I am not peeing in public."

"No one is out here. I'll keep an eye out for you."

"No fucking way, asshole."

"Well, what the hell, Karen? Are we supposed to just count the day a loss and quit looking for hag stones because you won't pee?"

"Call me Karen again and I will push your dumbass overboard while we are out to sea."

"Chill, bitch." He tried to say with a smirk and hint of teasing. But it didn't go over well with his wife.

"Fucking stay here with your fucking bullshit, asshat. I am going back to the ship to pee. You better change your stinking attitude before you come back to the room, or you will be going overboard for sure."

As she stormed off, Gary was silent. He knew he'd pushed her a bit too much with the Karen and bitch comments. He needed to learn to read her better. Or at least think before he spoke. Communication was the only real issue in the marriage, and it was always his fault due to miscommunication issues.

He waited until Katie rounded the corner of the beach and was out of view before he continued looking for the hag stones. He needed to make something good come of this. If he showed up with multiple stones in the room later, he might be able to appease Katie a little bit for his previous faux pas.

She will accept my diligence as an offering. I will bow before the queen with a gift of jewels.

Chapter Six

Morty hadn't moved in hours. It was just what the doctor ordered. R&R on a grand scale. No people. No work. Nothing but the sounds of waves and seagulls and the feel of the breeze and warm sun on his skin. Checking the time, he decided the gig was up. There was still adequate time to board, but he wanted to beat the crowds.

He left after the major ship exodus in the morning and wanted to return before everyone showed up to re-board the cruise. His day was well planned and proceeding according to his expectations.

Perfection.

When he got up from his prone position on the ground, he noticed a woman walking in his direction and heading towards the docked ship. He stood still. Shaking off sand, he watched her.

Katie watched him too. Silently, she was screaming in her mind. *He's death.* Somehow or other, her empathic abilities homed in on his true nature. Normally, her husband would point out reapers when he saw them. She could see them, but only as she got closer to them. From a distance, they all looked like normal people. Up close, she could see or sense the aura.

This one increased in visibility as she had crossed the beach in his direction. Now she was near enough to be paralyzed with fear. She stood still. While the aura was new, she thought she recognized him. *He's the same one we saw before, hovering with another reaper over that dead body. Is he here for me? Is it my time?*

Together, they stood on the beach staring at each other. Neither moving. Neither talking. It was a silent stand-off.

Why the hell won't she just keep going and get on the ship already? Morty tried desperately to figure out what was going on with this woman. He wanted to get back to the ship before everyone else. But he didn't want to get too close to her, whether it be in front of her or behind her.

There had already been some accidental deaths. The last thing he needed was a bizarre scenario and another angry reaper breathing down his neck. *I'll just have to wait. I still have almost two hours before the horn blows to tell everyone to come back to the ship.*

What is he doing? Why the hell isn't Gary right behind me? Of all the times for us to be separated, does it have to be now? With death just standing there staring at me? I'm not going to move. Maybe I'm not his target. Maybe it's just a coincidence. But is he on the cruise? Twice in one trip I've seen him. Since when does death take cruises?

Her mind raced with questions even as she cursed her situation as well as the pain and discomfort overcoming her. She didn't know anything about death, much less its process of selection and targeting. That was Gary's job. He was able to compartmentalize it for the most part and didn't bring work home with him. She never really asked. She didn't know if death had a process it had to follow. Was it random?

Fuck him. Move, asshole. My bladder hurts. But I'll be damned if I am going to stand here and piss myself. He doesn't deserve to think he has me terrified. Hold it, Katie. Hold it. He has to move at some point. He can't just stand there all day, can he?

Similar thoughts were occurring to Morty. He wondered why she was standing there and how long she would play the role of statue while staring at him. He started thinking she had some ulterior motive. *Maybe she's with accounting. Damn, is she investigating me?*

He wanted her to move and be about her business. But she stood like a pillar of stone. She didn't even seem to blink an eye. Minutes turned into an hour. Both stood still. Both lamented the situation. Neither of them had a plan of what to do next or how to get back to the ship without issues. Katie felt intense abdominal pain and pressure. She needed to pee so badly she was no longer in discomfort but intense physical pain from holding it in.

Morty knew the clock was ticking. He was running out of time before the horn would blow and the crowds would converge on the gangways to get back onto the ship. *Move, bitch. Just start walking already*, Morty thought.

Fucking asshole death fucking bastard motherfucking jerk. Go away. Go away now, Katie ranted to herself.

BACK ON THE ROCKS, Gary slipped, stumbled, and fell into a pool of water. Other than bruising his ego a little bit, no damage was done. He had a minor scrape on his right knee. He'd probably get a bruise or welt out of it. But it was worth it. In the pool of water were two hag stones.

He grabbed them one at a time and put them into the bag strapped around his shoulder and chest, where they had already placed the other one. Temporarily forgetting the pain, he smiled. His unfortunate footing had resulted in a wonderful accident of convenience. He might never have seen those hag stones had he not fallen in the pool in the first place.

A full day of looking around and I fall on my ass to find two. What's the odds of that happening? Katie will be happy. Now we'll have three we can sell in her oddities shop when we get home.

Climbing back up on the rocks, he decided it was time to go back to the ship. Katie was probably still fuming. But at least she would calm down now that she'd had a chance to pee. And returning with two additional hag stones would help pave his way to forgiveness. Of course, he planned on groveling as well. *Come bearing gifts. Come groveling. Surefire road to forgiveness.*

Climbing over rocks and carefully making his way to the sandy portion of the beach, he headed back in the direction of the ship. As he rounded the corner on the beach, he noticed Katie just standing still. Her silhouette was always immediately visible to him, even in crowds. While her back was to him, he knew even from a distance it was his wife.

Looking at her, he noticed another guy on the beach not far away from Katie. He was also standing still. And the dude was a reaper. He couldn't quite see his face. But the aura made it clear his wife was standing near a reaper. He wondered what the hell was happening. He stopped and watched for a few minutes. Neither his wife nor the reaper moved. *That's odd.*

He shook it off and figured he would ask her in person. He wondered if they were engaged in some sort of conversation he could not hear from his distance. But it seemed odd considering her previous level of discomfort and frantic need to urinate. Confused by it all, he started walking towards her and the ship.

Morty noticed the man approaching from his right. His plan to board the ship in relative isolation was falling apart. The ship's horn would blow soon, reminding guests it was time to board. And now he had two people near him. He needed the woman to leave and the man to just walk on by so he could try to get on the ship in a timely manner.

"Katie? What are you doing?" Gary shouted out as he got a little closer.

Well crap. They know each other. Now I'm going to be delayed even more. Just walk and talk. Walk and talk already. Don't stand there with her.

Katie did not move or answer. She gave no indication that she even heard him. Gritting her teeth and pushing against her abdomen, she tried to fight off the pain. It got so bad, she doubled over and fell to her knees before totally collapsing on the sand.

Gary saw Katie crumple and ran the final distance to her. Bending over her, he reached beneath her shoulders and lifted. He turned to look at the man standing there.

"Call for help!" He yelled.

Morty was dumbfounded. *What the hell is going on?*

Cradling her head against her chest and looking her over, Gary tried to find out what was wrong with his wife. She didn't seem to have any injuries. This reaper had not done anything to her as far as he could tell. But her eyes were rolled back in her head, and her breathing was shallow with too much time between inhaling and exhaling. It was labored and erratic.

"Katie, what's wrong?" Turning to look at the man standing there watching them, he yelled again. "CALL FOR HELP, ASSHOLE!"

Morty was shaken. He had been standing there taking it all in but was almost in a trance trying to put it all together. But the urgency in the man's voice shook him out of his stupor.

"Oh, I don't have a phone on me. I left it in the cabin so I could enjoy the day without interruptions."

Gary didn't seem to hear or pay attention to what he was saying.

"Katie! Katie! Stay with me, honey."

With a labored gasp and a final convulsion, she lay still. Checking for a pulse, Gary found none. He bent his head down so that his ear was right by her mouth and nose. He didn't hear or feel any breathing. In a panic, he started doing CPR.

The ship's warning horn blew. People started coming from multiple directions on the beaches and from the small town on Fargo Cay. Someone noticed Gary performing CPR and yelled for help. Others used their phones to call the ship's emergency number.

When the paramedics arrived, both Gary and Morty were overwhelmed. Gary because he had no idea what was going on with his wife. He was exhausted from giving CPR. He was confused. He was angry at the situation and angry with himself for their last conversation being somewhat quarrelsome.

Morty was overwhelmed because the crowds were building up near the ship gangways. A small crowd had gathered around the woman and her husband as well. Paramedics took over the CPR, checked for a pulse and breathing, and asked Gary how long this had been happening. Gary wasn't sure.

"I don't know. She just collapsed. I started CPR when I couldn't find a pulse and realized she wasn't breathing."

When CPR was not enough to do the trick, they used a portable automated external defibrillator. Applying electric shocks, they hoped to get her heart started and a good pulse going.

When the first couple of attempts failed, they raised the shock level from 120 to 200 joules. Maxing out the power of the portable device, they tried a few more times. Nothing happened. There was no pulse, and Katie was not breathing.

One of the paramedics pulled Gary aside. He already knew she was dead just from watching the rescue efforts and their lack of success with the defibrillator. The other paramedic waved off the crowd. Katie was dead, and they wanted to give the man some space and the lady who died some semblance of dignity without a gawking crowd hovering about her. While they did not know the cause of her predicament or death, there was nothing they could do to bring her back. It was up to the coroner now to find out what had happened to her.

The crowd on the beach dispersed in silence. Most had never seen someone die before. Somehow, the death of a fellow cruise line passenger right in front of them put a damper on their otherwise fabulous day ashore.

Morty waited for the crowd to leave and began his own slow walk towards the ship. The horn bellowed again. That was the fifteen-minute warning. The ship would be leaving whether he was on it or not. He had to make his way to the gangways and start boarding even though there were throngs of people converging at the same time.

He mentally crossed his fingers and moved forward. *Last thing I need is more trouble.*

Chapter Seven

Back on the ship, word spread quickly about the death on the beach. Gary was overwhelmed with grief.

"What the hell happened?" Gary asked them as they came out of the examination room, where his wife's body now lay deep within the bowels of the ship.

Gary was told that the ship doctor's initial review said there were no external wounds or injuries. Thinking it might have been a widow-maker heart attack, the doctor had ordered a precursory ultrasound. It wasn't the heart. Further tests, including cutting open her torso to investigate things properly, would have to be undertaken after they docked in Fort Lauderdale to end the cruise. At that point, they would engage with the Broward County Medical Examiner's office for a thorough investigation at a more capable facility. But they wanted to share the initial diagnosis with her husband.

"It's rare." The ship's doctor told him. He and the nurse on call stood together with Gary as they broke the news.

"We've never seen it on a cruise before. I've only personally heard of one other time when this has happened." The doctor said. "And this is just a preliminary diagnosis. We will have to have proper tests done and a coroner with better facilities verify our suspicions."

"Okay. I understand. It's not locked in stone. But give me something already. I just lost my wife and have no idea what happened. One minute she's standing there. The next one she collapses and dies."

"It is rare." He reiterated. "And you might want to get it verified one way or the other by the medical examiner back home."

"Fuckin' A, just tell me. You have my permission to order a proper autopsy once we dock in Fort Lauderdale. But for fuck's sake, spit it out already."

"She seems to have experienced a burst bladder. Once again, we would want to verify this and, if it is the case, we would also want to determine if there was something specific which caused it. But it appears that her bladder burst, and urine and the related toxins flooded into her abdominal cavity. Normally, this can be treated. Some cases require quick action and surgery. But even those can usually be treated successfully. The key is seeking immediate medical attention."

"Then why is she dead if it can be treated? She just collapsed."

"Unfortunately, that remains to be determined. I wish we could give you better answers. But we don't have the capabilities at this facility to do a deeper dive into the cause and results." The doctor said.

"Cause and results? RESULTS? The result is she is dead. DEAD!" Gary leaned against the wall, propping himself up with one arm. His grief and anger swelled into a maelstrom, which threatened to cause his body to collapse. He desperately tried to hold it together.

"She said she had to pee. I held her up before she headed back to the ship. This is my fault." Gary lamented.

He blamed himself. He shook visibly. He leaned against the corridor wall with his shoulder for additional support. Putting a hand on his shoulder, the ship's doctor tried to comfort him.

"This rupture didn't just happen when she collapsed. It had to have happened before. Tests might help us determine a timeline. But based on what we know of this kind of situation, it is likely the burst happened and was unnoticed. There is a good chance it went untreated for a long enough time that it caused multiple organs to fail."

Gary looked at him in shock.

"How could something like that go unnoticed? Wouldn't it cause crippling pain or have other side effects or symptoms? It doesn't make sense."

"We'll have to get a full report. I wish we could give you the timeline and details now, but we cannot. Normally, there would be severe pain and possibly some distension in the abdomen. Sometimes blood is visible in the urine. Did you notice these things at all?"

"She had pain and discomfort. But her belly wasn't swollen. And what pain she had was managed. It wasn't crippling, although we had discussed maybe not going out today if her discomfort level was too high. But she was fine this morning. And she didn't have any blood in her urine. At least not that she mentioned."

"Sometimes, the blood is only detectable with a test and not visible to the eye. Did she ever mention difficulty urinating, being nauseated and/or vomiting?"

"No. She didn't mention difficulty urinating. She did have to go more often than usual. But other than increased frequency and some discomfort, she didn't have issues. No nausea or vomiting either that I noticed or that she mentioned. Fuck. I should have paid more attention. This never would have happened. This is my fault."

The nurse piped in to help out. "It's no one's fault, these things just happen."

"It's my fault. Even though she was fine when we got off the ship today, I should have come back with her to make sure she got to the ship and a bathroom. She wouldn't pee out on the beach, even secluded behind boulders and trees. I was an ass. Now she's dead. It's my fault."

As the medical team tried to comfort him, Gary shook with anger. Shaking them off, he stormed towards the center of the ship to head back to his room. The doctor and nurse followed behind just in case he collapsed in his current condition. Gary saw Morty going up a glass elevator and to his room.

"No, it's his fault! He kept her from getting to the ship." His anger stoked, he ran to the center of the ship to try to see if he could determine the floor where Morty would get off the elevator. "You'll pay for this." He said loud enough for people around him to hear.

Chapter Eight

"Holy shit, Jim. You've done it now."

He had just picked up the phone and felt like he had walked into the middle of the conversation. Totally confused about what was going on now, he waited a second for more information from his boss.

"Heads will roll."

"What are you talking about, Joe? What am I missing? I thought we worked out all the kinks and discrepancies and gave accounting the happy-ending scenario they wanted."

"Are you serious? You don't know? Don't you monitor your team?"

"Of course I do. But I don't know what you are talking about, Joe."

"Morty is being accused of the unthinkable. If it is true, there's trouble brewing. Right now, only a few of us have any idea. But if it gets out, and he learns this news, shit will hit the fan in a big way."

"The unthinkable? What is that? I can't even imagine."

"He might have killed the wife of the new boss. Turns out they are on the same cruise, and now she is dead."

Jim's jaw dropped. He had nothing to say. He couldn't wrap his head around this news. *The wife of the new director for the western hemisphere? Holy shit, Morty, you've screwed us all now.*

"This is bad, Jim. Really bad."

"I don't even…"

"Nor do I. If you can get in touch with Morty, try to find out what happened. If we can get this cleared up and explained before word gets to Gary, we might survive. If not, all of us could be in for a hell of a ride. And it's not a ride we want to be on, Jim."

"No, it isn't. I'll see what I can find out. Keep me posted, please."

"I will. But keep this silent. The people who know owe me favors. They are willing to delay the findings to give us time, even if they determine Morty is guilty. It gives us a chance to find out the truth. But if he is guilty, it gives us a chance to build our own cases for protection from the inevitable fallout and consequences."

When Joe hung up, Jim ran to his bathroom and started throwing up into the toilet. This was a whole new level of stress and worry, the likes of which he had never experienced before.

Morty got off on the 13th floor and headed to his cabin. He had no idea anyone was watching him, much less blaming him for a death. What happened was weird. But it was obviously not his fault. He had not moved. He had not gotten near the woman at all. Her collapse and ultimate demise wasn't even an accident like his scythe beheading that guy. This was not on him. Not at all. No chance the bosses or accounting could blame him in any way.

He sat down on the couch in his cabin and turned on the television. Flipping channels, he found a paranormal ghost hunting show he thought he'd enjoy. He kicked off his shoes and leaned back on the couch while putting his feet on the coffee table in front of him.

The phone rang. *Oh, come on. WTF?* It was the boss. Again.

"Hey boss. What's happening? Did everything go okay with accounting? No one has contacted me about it. But I know the tale we agreed upon. The one you wanted me to use as a united front with the bean counters."

"Uh, yeah, everyone's pretty happy with that piece of things so far. At least accounting and the chain of command are happy as far as we can tell. Not everyone has seen the reports yet. But things are pretty good overall. The other team that has quotas and task orders for this region — well, that's another matter. They are unhappy. I'm sure the annual meeting will be a shitshow when they come across us. But we can worry about that at a later point."

"Okay, glad the main people are happy. We can deal with the others as necessary. There's a lot of time between now and the annual meeting. All will be well by then. Plenty of time for them to get their job done and let the current sting fade away."

"Yeah, but that's not why I called."

"Ok. So, what's up?"

"You created a bit of a problem with an unsanctioned kill."

"What are you talking about? I didn't kill anyone."

"The lady on the beach. Reports say her name was Katie. The problem is that she was not slated for death yet. Not even close. The records don't even show a projected date at this time. It is at least 5 years out based on forecasts. It could be even longer since the projections only go out five years at a time. And yet she is dead. And once again, the fingers are pointing at you."

"That had nothing to do with me. I saw her. I didn't move. Didn't go near her. She just stood there and collapsed. Next thing I knew, there were paramedics, and she was being declared dead. I. AM. INNOCENT."

"You can emphasize that all you want. And frankly, I kind of believe you. But that's neither here nor there. This is an unsanctioned and unplanned death. It has to be handled. Somehow."

"Come on, boss. What the hell? I didn't do anything."

"The investigators think differently. Their review indicates that you delayed her unnecessarily and caused her demise. They think if you had walked away, she would still be alive, and her demise would not have happened now. For that matter, she'd still be alive for at least five more years."

"Well, shit. Now what? This is B.S. if you ask me. How the hell would investigators even know this already much less have come to such a conclusion? I mean, she just died. Again, this is total B.S. if you ask me."

"I didn't ask you, Morty. I am telling you. You've created an issue. There is no existing protocol for this situation. Right now, legal is meeting with accounting. The oversight board is reviewing the investigators' reports to determine if any disciplinary action will be required. As for the how, who the hell knows? These investigators see damn near everything. They are omnipresent and powerful, even if not omniscient. But disciplinary action is not only a possibility, but at this point a likelihood. Maybe even the beginning of even worse things."

"Disciplinary action? For standing still and minding my own business? While I am on vacation? Why aren't you protecting me? This isn't how a good boss treats his staff."

"Don't get snarky and uppity with me. You have no idea what I am already doing to protect and shield you. I could just as easily roll you under the bus and play the role of Pilate, totally washing my hands of you. As for how they know or came to any conclusions, well, your activity has put them on alert. You are being watched and monitored. Every move you make is being meticulously studied and notated right now. I can't hold back the tide anymore."

Morty sat silently digesting what Jim had just told him. He decided it was not worth pushing his luck any further. Before he could apologize, a knock came at his stateroom door.

"What's that?"

"Oh, someone is at the door. I don't know. I didn't order any food or drinks. Could just be a courtesy call from the concierge staff handling the cabins on this floor."

"Okay, go take care of whatever they want. I'll check in with other folks and see where and how things are progressing. Then we'll get back together to discuss a plan of action. Meaning—you'll do whatever the fuck I tell you to do. Capisce?"

"Yes, sir." Morty and Jim hung up simultaneously.

While Morty sat still for a second trying to understand what was happening, the knocking at the door became more persistent. Louder. It was almost angry, if door knocking could sound angry.

He stared at the door from his position on the couch. The banging continued nonstop for a few minutes. Then it abruptly stopped, and there was silence.

Outside the door, Gary stood still. Frustrated. He knew that the dude who killed his wife got off on the 13th floor. He knew he was a reaper. But from his vantage point below, he was only able to tell which direction he walked after getting off the lift. He didn't know which room he went into afterwards.

He hadn't really paid attention to him the previous times he had seen him. He might not recognize his face in a big crowd. But that wouldn't matter. He had seen his aura before at the beginning of the cruise. He was a Reaper. He'd recognize him even if the face didn't stand out in his memory. The aura would be there.

I will find this bastard. And he will pay for killing Katie. And if he is in my directorate, the wrath will continue with his bosses and team. Everyone and anyone involved will pay for this.

Stopping to take a few deep breaths and regain his composure, Gary prepared to go to the next room. He slowly took the seven steps between doors with growing anticipation of finding his prey, his wife's killer. Revenge would be his.

When he heard the muffled knocking, Morty assumed that whoever had been at his door had figured out they were in the wrong place and moved on to another cabin. He relaxed a bit from the tension that had built up inside him from the combination of the phone call with Jim and the crazy and angry pounding on the door.

Whatever was going on, that person realized their mistake. *Probably drunk. Wife probably locked him out for bad behavior. Now he's banging on the door until she lets him in again.* Satisfied with his thoughts, he looked back at the television to watch the show he had found previously.

What a crazy ending to what had been an amazing day of relaxation!

The next port of call would be in Nassau. He planned on making a trip out to Fort Montague while most of the cruise line passengers would make their way to bars, look for some good cheap shopping, souvenirs, and tchotchkes, or get into the local cuisine.

While jerk chicken sounded amazing, his last attempt at ordering a special Mango Jerk Chicken had turned disastrous.

He'd pass. He figured it would be better to just go out and explore the fort to kill time before they headed back home. It was his last chance for an outing.

Chapter Nine

Sitting in her cabin reading a book while her husband was at the ship casino, Amanda was startled by the incessant knocking on her door. Taken aback, she dropped her book at the unexpected interruption. It wasn't the normal and peaceful knocking of the concierge team or butler. This was loud. Violent. Manic. Crazy and scary.

What the hell is going on? Where is Ray when I need him?

Her heart raced as she listened and watched the door. In her imagination, the door was bowing in with every beat from the outside. She knew that wasn't possible. But the terror was magnifying with each frantic round of banging. She started visualizing the door bursting open under the pressure of the incessant and violent banging.

"OPEN THE DOOR! I KNOW YOU'RE IN THERE! YOU WILL PAY!" Gary yelled.

Amanda had no idea who that was. The voice was unfamiliar. So many odd things ran through her mind. *Was her husband in trouble because of gambling? Had he pissed someone off to such an extent they'd come to his cabin looking for him? How would they even know what cabin they were in anyway? Did he owe a debt? What did he need to pay?*

Scared and uncertain about what was happening, Amanda sent a text to her husband.

"Ray, help. Someone is trying to get into the room. I don't know what's happening. Please God hurry."

She hoped Ray would see her text and come to her rescue. But in the meantime, she needed to do something to protect herself.

As the seconds turned into several minutes, she picked up the phone on the table next to her to call the concierge team. Her fear was growing exponentially. She needed help, and there was no telling when Ira would be returning to the cabin.

"Yes, Mrs. Resnit, what can we do for you?" A female voice asked from the other end as soon as she picked up the receiver.

"Someone's trying to get into my room. Please get security up here."

"What?" The lady who answered could tell that there was a serious sense of urgency and fear in Mrs. Resnit's voice. "Yes ma'am. I will call them now, and we will also come up to check on you."

"Please hurry."

"Yes, ma'am." She said with an urgency of her own when she heard yelling and banging through the phone Mrs. Resnit was holding.

Amanda Resnit fell to the ground in a panic. Her heart was beating so hard she felt like she could hear it. She crawled towards the bedroom of the cabin to get her nitroglycerine. Her breathing was labored. She knew the signs. The strain on her heart increased the chest pain. Her left arm started going numb. She needed her meds to open her blood vessels and get the flow going more smoothly.

She could hear the man beating on the door and yelling as she crawled from the sitting area to the bedroom. *Where is Ray? Where is security? Oh God, I need help, and I need it fast.* When she got into the bedroom and reached up to the nightstand where she kept all of her medication, the banging stopped.

Gary tired of this room. No one was there. Not a sound coming through the door. No response to his banging and yelling. It had to have been empty. If it was occupied, he would have had some response from the inhabitants to determine if it were his wife's killer.

With nothing happening, he quit banging. It was time to go to the next room. The bastard who killed his wife had to be up here somewhere. Soon he would find him and exact the retribution that jerk deserved. *I will find you, asshole. I. WILL. FIND. YOU.*

He gathered himself with renewed determination and anger. He wanted to pulverize his intended victim. He needed to keep the fire burning so he could unleash it on his intended victim.

As he was playing blackjack, Ray noticed his phone light up next to him. Picking it up he saw he had a text from his wife Amanda. *WTF? She knows I'm down here. I told her I wouldn't be back for a couple hours.*

Putting the phone down without unlocking it and reading the text, Ray continued with the hand of blackjack. After losing that hand and two more games to the dealer, he decided to take a break. Remembering he had a text from Amanda, he opened it up to see what she wanted. He was taken aback when he read it: "*Ray, help. Someone is trying to get into the room. I don't know what's happening. Please God hurry.*"

In a panic, Ray ran out of the casino floor and to the elevators to get to his wife. *WTF is going on?*

Chapter Ten

Gary was getting ready to start knocking on the next door but stopped because dropped his phone. He bent down to pick it up just as a security officer entered the hallway where he was located. Seeing the security guard just down the hall and not wanting to draw attention to himself, he calmly walked towards him like nothing was happening. The security guard nodded but was focused on getting to the room in question. Gary continued walking away, thinking about the revenge he intended to get.

Saved by the bell, asshole. But I'll be watching for you. You will pay the price for your crime. Your sin will be punished without mercy or forgiveness. This will be resolved to my satisfaction.

After passing the security guard, Gary turned around to watch what was happening. If the guard was just walking through making his rounds, he could go back to that room and continue his search for his wife's murderer.

Ray was agitated when the elevator stopped on the 5th floor. He was clenching his hands and grinding his teeth in frustration as people got on to the elevator with him. He recognized one of them as part of the concierge team working to serve the clients on his floor.

Relieved when the elevator door shut and continued it's journey, sweat beaded on his forehead. He couldn't get to Amanda soon enough to suit him. He started feeling guilty that he'd continued playing blackjack while his wife was expecting him to come help her.

Gary watched as the security guard stopped at the room he had previously attempted. He noticed the knocking and wondered if someone was actually in that room. When Gary heard the ping of the elevator, he looked in that direction and noticed people coming around the corner and into the hallway where he and security guard were already location.

Ray pushed past the others and hurried to his cabin to check on his wife. He saw the security guard there and started to question him when the guard spoke to the concierge team behind him.

"No answer. Are you sure this is the right room?"

"Yes, Mrs. Resnit called us from here. It's all tracked in the system. No mistaking it."

"What the fuck is going on!" Ray bellowed. "Get out of the way and let me get to my wife."

Fumbling for his room key, he dropped his wallet in panic. On his knees he couldn't find the key. The security guard knocked some more and called out, indicating he was with ship security and responding to her distress call. No response came. The door did not open.

"Open it." He told the concierge team while Ray continued trying to find his own key. Using their master pass key which was normally for making beds, restocking drinks, and other butler-related services, they opened the door.

They all entered the cabin, with the security guard going first. Ray gathered his wallet and ran in behind the security guard.

"Mrs. Resnit?" The concierge called out. "It's okay. Whoever was at the door is not there anymore. And we have security with us."

They looked towards the bedroom and bathroom area expecting the passenger to come out, even if sheepishly, now that she was safe. There was no movement. Ray ran past them and into the bedroom area. He found his wife Amanda lying on the floor.

"Call the doctor's office now." The security guard ordered.

Ray cradled his wife in his arms and rocked back and forth sobbing uncontrollably.

"Amanda. Come back to me. Come back to me."

SEEING THE MAN GO into the room with security in search of a woman, Gary knew he had the wrong room. His search for the killer would have to continue when things calmed down. In frustration, he walked around the other corner and towards the elevator banks.

He needed a stiff drink. He would go downstairs to one of the bars and figure out his next steps. Revenge would have to wait. Karma was slow. But it was coming.

Chapter Eleven

When he realized all the banging had stopped, Morty ventured to look out into the hallway. He couldn't see anything through the peephole. But he thought he heard a voice. It wasn't yelling anymore. Half-heartedly, he decided to open the door and look.

Perhaps if the drunk guy was still standing there, his appearance would scare him away. That might ensure a cessation of the noise activity in the hallway. Or perhaps the guy's wife had opened the door to let him in, and they were talking through it. In that case, just showing up might embarrass them enough to make them retire into their cabin to continue their discussions.

Unlocking the door slowly and listening for any loud voices or noises before he opened it, Morty took a deep breath. *Here goes nothing.* When he opened the door and walked out, the security guard was standing a couple of doors down and facing his direction in the hall while he talked to some other people.

"Hey, you!" he called out at Morty.

Surprised, Morty looked behind him as if perhaps someone else was in the hall and garnering the attention of the security guard. When he saw nothing, he sighed. His shoulders slackened, and he turned around sheepishly, replying. "Who, me?"

"Yeah, you. Is that your cabin?"

"Yes sir. Is there a problem?"

"Did you hear any banging or screaming or notice any kind of fracas going on in this wing?"

"Well, there was noise. But I didn't see anything. I was in my cabin. You just saw me come out."

"What noise?"

"Like you said. Banging. Screaming."

"What was the screaming about?"

"From what I heard, some dude was looking for someone and demanding they come and open the door. Something about a payback."

"That's similar to what Mrs. Resnit said when she called us." The lady who had taken the call in the concierge office said.

Ignoring her, the security guard stared at Morty.

"Pay back for what?"

"How should I know? I was in my cabin watching TV and relaxing. He beat on my door for a while and then moved on to my neighbor's door. Why are you asking me?"

"Mrs. Resnit called, as you just heard, complaining about banging. It scared her. I was asked to investigate."

"Okay, so what did you find out? I assumed her husband was drunk out of his mind and they had a fight, resulting in locking him out of the cabin. I figured he was so drunk that he didn't even know which cabin was which when he started knocking on mine."

"It wasn't her husband."

"Who was it? What is going on?"

"That's all for now, sir. If I have any more questions or need a statement, I'll be back."

Morty was a little frustrated being grilled like he was an accomplice to some great crime caper. But he was glad that the noise had ended and hoped they would get it all sorted out.

He stood there and watched thing unfold even though the security guard had turned his back to him. He heard the ping of the elevator doors and watched as the as team of medics rounded the corner and walked towards the cabin where everyone was gathered. The doctor walked past Morty without a thought and headed towards where the security guard was standing. The nurse, however, saw Morty in a different light.

She screamed and ran back towards the elevator. The doors were already closing, but she thrust her left arm in to stop them. The automatic safety sensors, which would open the doors in case of an obstruction, did not work. Her left arm was caught.

Screaming for help, she dropped to the floor as the elevator started going down. The others ran to her. The doctor was pushing buttons in a misguided attempt to stop the elevator.

The emergency stop button was inside the elevator. He didn't have the ability to stop it from the outside.

The nurse screamed as the elevator groaned, trying to go down. The weight of the lift cut through her arm. Blood shot out of her with a force like a fire hydrant as she experienced the amputation. The elevator doors, walls, and floor in front of it were covered in a spray of blood that seemed endless.

The concierge team was screaming. Morty stood dumbfounded at what had just happened. The ship's doctor and the concierge team stood frozen at the sight of so much blood spraying out of the nurse. No one knew what to do as she lay bleeding out.

The security guard was the first to get over his initial shock and took off his belt. He wrapped it around the stump of her arm, near the shoulder, to try to stem the bleeding. The notch holes in his belt were for a man. Wearing a size 44 pair of pants, the belt was too big to fasten via the normal methods on the nurse's arm. So, he tied it in a knot as tight as he could and called on his walkie-talkie for backup help and engineering.

AFTER LEAVING THE AREA, Gary headed down the elevators to the promenade deck to get something to drink. He fumed about the day that lay behind him. His wife died. Her killer was walking about as if nothing happened. He couldn't find the bastard. And evening was falling.

The ship had already been out to sea for a little while on its way to the final stop in Nassau before heading back to the port in Fort. Lauderdale, where his wife would be transported to the county medical examiner for a proper autopsy and preparation for shipment home for burial. When he got off the elevator on the promenade deck, he remembered his phone.

Taking his phone back out of his pocket, he double-checked to make sure he had not cracked the screen when he dropped it. As he looked, he noticed he had a couple of missed calls and additional voicemail notifications. He stepped out of the path of others entering and exiting the elevators and unlocked the phone. All the voice messages and missed calls came from the company.

He didn't have time for them. There were other things to focus on right now. He'd deal with them after the cruise. They had all been given orders to leave him and Katie alone while they got some downtime on this cruise. But they wouldn't. *I'll handle this shit when I get home.*

Putting his phone back in his pocket, he started walking away when he heard screaming. He turned around to see what the commotion was all about.

When the nurse's elevator reached the main promenade deck with the doors streaked in blood and a severed arm inside of it, those waiting for the lift started screaming. A few even fainted. The call had already gone out to both security and maintenance. But it was too late to avoid this public spectacle.

Gary watched as guards appeared and started to block off the area from view. But too many people had witnessed the arrival of the severed arm. News spread quickly throughout the ship.

Chapter Twelve

The doctor stopped working on the nurse and looked up at the concierge team and security guard with tears in his eyes. Between the severity of her wounds and the ineffectiveness of the security guard's belt, the nurse died from the trauma and blood loss before he could do anything. As news spread quickly throughout the ship, the captain was getting briefed by security.

He was worried. This could blow up to be even worse than the Poop Cruise. This could easily be called the Death Cruise and cripple the cruise line's business. The last thing they needed were viral videos.

"Get this cleaned up now!" The captain ordered. "No blood. Replace the carpet if you have to do so. Close that elevator.

Get all the bodies ready to depart the ship discreetly when we get back to Florida. No cameras. No audio. No one record anything. In fact, do security sweeps before removing the bodies from the ship. Get them out of here and to the county coroner's office without anyone knowing what's being transported. Get it done under cover of darkness after we arrive and hours before the guests are scheduled to leave."

No one argued. But they all knew it would be damn near impossible. The husbands of two of the deceased women would have to know the plan for removal. They were unlikely to care about any vow of secrecy. They were between a rock and a hard place but figured they would do their best, with each department involved working diligently to make things happen.

They all knew the consequences. The captain would not hesitate to fire people and keep them from working on this cruise line ever again. They also all knew that only two days remained on the cruise. The stop in Nassau and then the return to Ft. Lauderdale to end the cruise.

RAY WAS INFORMED BY the doctor that Amanda's death was ruled a massive heart attack. He nodded. "She was on meds. She was trying to get to them but didn't make it." Sobbing, he knew the doctor was right. Her heart had given out. He shook uncontrollably in a combination of grief and guilt. *This is all my fault. I should have read the text and come here immediately.*

"It's all my fault." He said pleadingly into the face of the doctor.

He was comforted and reassured that he could not have stopped the heart attack. It was little consolation. The love of his life was gone, and he thought it was because of him. He ignored the only person who mattered in his life. They gently helped Ray stand and sit on the bed.

Then they prepared to move Amanda's body to a waiting area for removal. When they got to port in Fort Lauderdale, she would be taken out along with Katie before the gangways were opened to the cruise ship passengers. They'd be moved through a service entrance.

Ray was offered the chance to accompany her body to the morgue holding area but refused to move. Instead, he sat in his room in silence for several hours before using the Wi-Fi to call his adult children and others in the family. Losing her was hard and unexpected. Explaining it to the children was more than he could take. After finishing the last call, he rolled into a fetal position on the floor in his cabin and started bawling.

Chapter Thirteen

Sitting at home relaxing and watching a movie, Jim tried to get the recent events out of his mind. When his phone rang with a call from Joe, there was no surprise. Jim expected it. Word spread quickly throughout the cruise ship, but more disturbingly, throughout the organization. A nurse had been dismembered. Another totally unsanctioned death had taken place on Morty's vacation.

"We haven't sorted out the other messes yet, and Morty kills again?" Joe was so irate, he dropped the phone. Jim's seconds of reprieve ended with a new tirade when his boss picked the phone back up.

After being harangued for nearly 5 minutes non-stop, Jim was worried about where the conversation would go next. Joe took a deep breath. More calmly, he asked, "what do we do now, Jim?"

Hearing the plea in Joe's voice, he knew things had escalated to new levels of crazy in the organization.

"From what I hear, boss, she got trapped in an elevator somehow. Morty didn't do anything."

"It's always this way with you. Defending Morty. Saying he's innocent. The bean counters don't think so. Gary isn't going to think so considering his wife is one of the victims of Morty's vacation antics."

"I'm sure all these accidents can be explained. There must be protocols for when an accident happens."

"Protocols for when an accident happens? Is that what you dared say to me, Jim? Oh, there are definitely protocols for when AN. ACCIDENT. HAPPENS. There are no protocols for a constant stream of accidents. This vacation and the resulting accidents are all unprecedented. No one knows how to deal with anything. You know what that means? Do you?"

"No sir. Trouble, I presume?"

"Trouble you presume? You have no frickin' idea. Several departments, including legal, accounting, and forecasting, are all placing calls to Gary. There is no hope of the new boss not knowing or finding out what's going on and how his wife died on our watch along with several others. We'll be lucky to keep our lives, much less our jobs, when this purge is over. Shit is going to hit the fan big time."

"What now? I don't know what to do," Jim asked, trembling.

"No one knows what to do. What part of unprecedented do you not understand? Add in the totally unknown factor of how the new boss might respond. At least with the old boss, we would have had some rough idea of what to expect. Now we are going in blind. But this is where we are going to start. Tell Morty that's it. Vacation over. He is to remain in his cabin for the rest of the cruise. He is not to order food or leave his cabin until told to do so. We will work on trying to get him out unseen by anyone either before or after the other passengers. But he is to remain isolated and out of sight and contact with anyone on that ship until told otherwise. Do you understand?"

"Yes, sir."

"Get him on the phone as soon as we hang up. There can be no additional issues. It has to be nipped in the bud now, although I suspect it is already too late. Even so, we can try to keep it from escalating to something even worse." Joe hung up the phone when he finished his sentence.

Keep it from getting worse? How could it get worse? We'll be lucky to survive at all.

As soon as that conversation was over, he immediately di aled. Joe was already mid-sentence before Morty had the phone fully to his ear. "... furthermore, you will not leave the ship until told to do so."

"Um, okay, I guess. What's the story now? I was planning on going out to Fort Montague and exploring tomorrow after we stop in Nassau, and most of the other guests are already off the ship."

"No. You. Will. Not. Stay put in your cabin. Period. Stay put. Period. Stay put. Period. Do I need to tell you again? Get this through your thick skull; we have lost control of the situation altogether. We are in panic mode and crisis management right now. The best we can do is alleviate or mitigate some of the coming consequences."

"Oh shit. This has turned out to be a terrible vacation. What little time I've had to enjoy things keeps getting interrupted. Now I have to basically be on house arrest until Ft. Lauderdale?

This is B.S. on a grand scale. And all because of stupid accidents that didn't involve me."

"Didn't involve you? I wish we could spin that. I really do. But that's not how things are going down. And we still have no idea what will happen when Gary finds out that you killed his wife ahead of schedule. Far ahead of schedule. Unsanctioned. There's not much chance he will care if it was an accident. On top of that, it appears no one has actually talked to him yet. So, he doesn't know about the other deaths. It's going to blow the hell up if he thinks you not only killed his wife but went on a killing spree without any authorization, stole scheduled kills from others, and were responsible for ones like Katie that were not even forecasted to die and for whom no task orders went out. He has access to most of this stuff even if he is not allowed information on himself or Katie for timing. He can look up the other ones like your cabin neighbor Amanda Resnit."

"What the hell? You know I had nothing to do with any of this."

"Who cares what you think or what I think. Shit is blowing up. Perception is stronger than fact. So, I repeat, you will not leave the ship until told to do so. Do you understand that?"

"Yes."

"Furthermore, you are not to order food or drink. Live off whatever is in your cabin, fruits, drinks in the fridge, etc. Stay put."

"Ok."

Morty fumed after the conversation. Vacation became house arrest. House arrest may in turn morph into much worse consequences. And all because he demanded an unprecedented vacation for a reaper position. He'd have been better off putting in his work time and collecting souls and fulfilling his assignments.

Chapter Fourteen

Upon stopping in Nassau, Gary was standing ready at the gangway on Deck 2 which would be used by all departing passengers for the day. He'd get out with the first handful of people and take up a position to watch for his wife's killer as he got off the ship.

As the minutes turned into hours, his frustration grew. People came off the ship in a steady stream for the first couple of hours. But after that, it was a trickle. A handful of people at a time coming out in small groups of two or three with their traveling companions. But his wife's killer was not one of them.

When no one had left the ship in more than an hour, Gary gave up. *Maybe he isn't coming out today. Bastard. I'll give up this watch but come back down later at the end of the day to see if he eventually leaves and I can spot him returning when the whistle blows.*

With his mind made up, Gary returned to the ship and headed up to his cabin. As he walked in, the phone on the end table in his sitting area was ringing. He answered the unexpected call. He nodded his head and muttered his assent as the ship's doctor explained to him the process for his wife's removal in Fort Lauderdale the next morning. They would be taking her off the ship early to avoid any public spectacle for his and his wife's sake.

While he appreciated their discretion, the news only fueled his anger. One night. That's all that was left to get this guy if he wanted him before docking in Fort Lauderdale. If he and his wife were being transported early, he wouldn't have the chance to wait for him to get off the ship back in Florida.

It had to be tonight. He had to pay before the final stop or potentially slip away into the crowds with no consequences for his actions. *That will not do. He will pay.*

As HIS PHONE RANG again, Joe was a little scared. Things had gotten seriously out of hand. He relayed all this to Morty and ordered him not to leave his cabin. So, the ringing of his phone made him worry that Morty had left the cabin and done something stupid. With growing dread and apprehension, he picked up his cell phone to answer.

"Yes?"

"Joe, this is Jim."

I already knew that, dumbass. Caller ID is a real thing. But my ringtone for you also lets me know what's up without even looking at the phone. Asshole line 1. Asshole line 1.

"Oh, hi Jim. I wasn't expecting you to call. Just so you know, I have had the come to Jesus talk with Morty. He understands he is not to leave that cabin without orders. Furthermore, he is not even allowed to order food or drinks delivered to his room. He is essentially on house arrest from my perspective."

"Good. But that's not what I called about."

"Okay, I hope it isn't another accusation or accidental death of some sort."

"Not at all. But it is about the whole situation. On the one hand, no one has talked to Gary yet. Keep in mind he has been left voice messages. Whether he has listened to them or not is unknown. He has not responded to them. But on the other hand, department meetings are coming back with different feedback. Accounting is looking at these numbers and feeling good about Morty's work. Investigators feel similarly, although they do not want to potentially get in the crossfire when Gary makes his appearance in this situation."

"What about forecasting or marketing?"

"Interestingly, marketing is loving it. They are working on recruiting slogans, if you can believe that. The favored one right now is: 'Join the team and you can even reap while on vacation.' Forecasting has mixed feelings. On the one hand, you are screwing up their predictions with deaths happening before they should. The ones that are off by minutes or hours aren't that big a deal. Ones like Katie are worrying them. It makes them look bad if someone is not on the forecast but gets reaped."

"This sounds less panicked than previous conversations."

"It is. For now, anyway. Things are moderately leaning in our direction. There's even discussion going around about promoting Morty or putting him in charge of training regimens."

"Promotion? Or training? WTF Joe? One minute my head's damn near on a chopping block because of Morty and the next minute you're talking about promoting him?"

"Yes, I know. Things are fluid here and moving quickly. Anything could happen. But if we can pull off the latter; it will be a boon for all of us. But the wild card is still out there."

"Gary?"

"Of course, idiot. The new boss has considerable pull and power. Right now, his anger is boiling over the loss of his wife. No one knows how he will react. Unfortunately, the cruise is almost over. That means he will soon be confronted with questions even if he doesn't listen to his voicemail. How he responds to being bombarded with questions about forecasting, unsanctioned kills, and stealing reapings from other teams could be a deadly combination when mixed with his current state of mind."

"So, what now?"

"Nothing really. Just sit still and make sure Morty does the same. The less anyone hears his name right now, the better. We need as much time and silence as we can buy. Then we cross our fingers and hope for the best. If the other departments fully pull in our favor, they may be able to offset Gary's anger. If not... I hesitate to think about it in detail."

"Wow. Okay."

After relaying that conversation to Morty, Jim waited for a response.

"Is this real? A promotion of some sort? For doing nothing?" Morty thought it was a joke.

"It is only one possibility. Other possibilities are much worse."

"So, now I just wait for the call to get off the ship and sit around twiddling my thumbs?"

"You got it. We are in waiting mode right now. Stay put until you get further instructions."

"Yes, sir."

Chapter Fifteen

After talking to the ship's doctor and getting briefed on the plans for his wife's removal from the ship, Gary sat down and wept. For the first time, he allowed his grief to overtake his anger and desire for revenge. After nearly an hour of weeping, he felt exhausted, but a little relieved.

He grabbed a soda from the fridge in his cabin and noticed his phone on the table. He picked it up. *This is as good a time as any to see why they keep calling me.* He started listening to his messages.

The ship's doctor got in touch with Ray Resnit next. He was also informed as to the process for removing his wife from the ship and transporting her to the coroner with minimal eyes, privacy, and dignity. He appreciated their concern for discretion but wondered if it really made any difference at this point. The love of his life was gone. Discretion would not bring her back.

After hanging up the phone, Mr. Resnit collapsed on his bed. Once again, he rolled himself into a fetal position. Mourning turned to desperation. *How can I live without her? Why even bother? She should have outlived me. That's the way it is supposed to be. Not like this. I can't take this pain and loss. I can't go on without her.*

Bawling uncontrollably, Ray Resnit's energy was expended to the point he fell asleep still in a fetal position and thinking about death.

IN HIS OWN CABIN, Gary started listening to the voice messages, and his anger started growing again. Unsanctioned killings, timeline issues, and a rogue reaper on the loose. So, when he had seen this reaper on the pier with another reaper and a dead person, it was a stolen job. This guy not only killed his wife but also stole an assignment from another team. Something else he'd have to deal with when he got back.

How many stinking people did this guy kill? This jerk is supposed to be on a one-of-a-kind, unprecedented vacation, and he's out reaping willy-nilly. Heads will roll. I will call these people back and deal with all this crap after the cruise.

For now, there remains only one thing to be done. Make this rogue reaper pay for Katie's death. Then I can worry about accounting and the other teams who are pissed off. For now, death is coming for you, reaper. Your vacation is about to end.

As late afternoon approached, Gary knew he needed to get back down to the piers to watch for this rogue reaper named Morty. He knew the face. Now he had a name. It would give him a little extra pleasure in calling him by name when he confronted him for killing his wife.

Morty sat in his cabin brooding. The vacation he needed turned into nothing more than hiding and confinement. He figured he'd have been better off going about his daily and monotonous routine of reaping. Although he was glad, he didn't have to hear people plead for more time, for one more chance, for an opportunity to say goodbye to someone they loved.

The groveling got old. He was just there to do a job, not take confessions or give comfort. People just didn't understand. He was basically a repo man. He wondered if regular repo men went through the same kind of crap when picking up a car or appliances or whatever was on their task order for the day.

With boredom and frustration overtaking him, he decided to sit out on the deck. The cool Caribbean breeze and sounds could at least help him relax a little bit. The sea looked calm and sparkled in the sun. As the hours passed by, he fell asleep, dreaming of quiet sandy beaches and solitude.

Ray had passed out in the fetal position. The energy of sobbing and the overwhelming weight of mourning and sadness had shut his body down. But his mind still raced. Even in his dreams. He woke up in a sweat as the nightmares and fear overwhelmed him in his sleep. Getting up to take a shower and clean up from the sweat and tears, he turned on Calypso music and cranked the shower up to steaming hot.

After he was done cleaning, he just stood in the shower as tears mixed with streams of hot water, washing them down the drain. He watched the water swirl around the drain a little bit. He realized his life had spun out of control and was going down the drain. It needed to end.

Getting out of the shower, drying, and getting dressed, he sat on the bed wondering what he should do. The ship would not dock until the morning. He didn't know what he was going to do other than try to sleep during the night. But even once docked and Amanda's body was removed from the ship, he didn't know what he'd do. He had no reason to live. She was his everything. Now she was gone. As bad as it was now, it was only going to get worse.

He picked up the phone and dialed 988. He knew that was the new number for the veterans crisis/suicide helpline. Something had to give. He was reaching for some semblance of hope and help as the phone rang.

Gary made his way down the elevator to the gangway. As he got off on level 3 and headed towards the exit, he curled his fists. His anger grew with each step. He was going to kill this bastard one way or the other. He figured his position would enable his support teams to cover things up for the most part, justify his actions, and sway any negative consequences.

Then he would deal with all the other issues in his new responsibilities in his hemisphere. He had visions of the labors of Hercules and when he diverted the and Peneus rivers to clean the stables. *Yeah. I'm going to clean house. The filth of these stables will be washed away in my wrath.*

Screaming woke Morty up from his nap on the deck. Jumping up, he tried to determine where the noise was coming from and what was happening. *Oh God, please no. Not again. I can't even sleep in peace.*

The next set of screams drew his attention outward and down to the sea. *Whew. Just some young folks playing around on jet skis. Harmless fun. No harm, no foul.*

Outside the ship, Gary paced back and forth. He kept a vigilant eye on the people returning to the ship. He knew the whistle would blow soon. Then more people would be returning in haste to get on the ship. He might have missed Morty in the morning.

He would not miss his returning. He began to get antsy. Nervous. He started sweating as his anxiety and anger combined into a whirlwind of emotions. "Olly oxen free," he found himself speaking aloud without thinking.

AFTER DIALING 988, RAY waited for someone to answer. On the third ring, he was connected. He wondered why something like a major crisis line took three rings. He thought it should be automatic – not even a full ring – just an automatic source of help on the other end. It was a crisis and suicide line after all and not some help desk request being rerouted to a call center in Bangladesh.

The greeting on the other end was automated. *A fuckin' machine?* The message was asking if he needed specialized support. Did he want the Veteran's crisis line? Did he want Spanish speaking services?

What the hell? Crisis line my ass. I might as well try to get the IRS on the phone and walk through issues. "Fucking ridiculous". He said as he ended the call. *Why even bother? It's obvious I am not supposed to be here anymore. Without Amanda, nothing matters.*

Chapter Sixteen

The first warning horn blew. Gary watched. The crowds had already begun returning to the ship. His ability to watch for specific faces was being challenged by the throngs. If Morty thought a press of people would help him get around incognito, however, he was sadly mistaken.

Gary might not know his face well, but he had the sight. He could spot a reaper. He would see him even if he was blocked by other people. His unique aura would stand out. So, he waited and watched. Not bothering to focus on the faces which were becoming blurred and blocked, he watched for the tell-tale aura of the reaper who had killed his wife.

Relieved that no one had killed themselves or accidentally died, Morty relaxed. The screams that had woken him had startled him and pushed his fear and anxiety to a boiling point, worrying about another unsanctioned, unauthorized, or worse, un-forecasted reaping. That would be the last thing he needed now. The sounds outside on the water continued. But they became white noise for him since he knew what they were.

Going to the fridge, he pulled out some leftovers and a soda he had in there. A little boring microwaved pile of leftovers was better than nothing. But just barely. He hated his confinement and couldn't wait to be given the order to get off the ship. The mango jerk chicken he'd dreamed about was not going to bless his palate. *This vacation sucks.*

Gary made his way slowly towards a little higher vantage point. Stone walls lined the pier towards the aft of the ship. He figured he could get up on one of them. Being a few feet higher than the returning cruise line passengers would give him a better vantage point for spotting Morty. He climbed up easily enough and stood there. He watched.

Ray left his cabin. Sobbing and shaking with grief and anger, he got on the elevator to go up to the promenade deck for some air. He thought the breeze, the sounds of music, and laughter might help him where the automated crap of 988 was useless.

Walking around the ship, he looked for a place he could moderately be alone. He wanted to hear and see things. But he didn't want to interact with anyone.

He thought about his life without Amanda. He didn't see how he could bother going on anymore. She was his life. He began to understand why couples often died together or very close to each other in time. The grief for some was overwhelming. Now he knew. Firsthand.

A couple was walking around a corner near him. Entering the promenade deck from another hallway connected to elevators in the aft portion of the ship, they came out in the middle of an argument which had started on the elevator. Ray had no idea what the argument was about. But he felt the anger and vitriol in his bones when he heard the woman say, "Why don't you just fucking die!" towards the man.

He turned quickly to look at her.

The couple saw him turn. "Sorry about that. We should take our conversation back to the room." The man said.

"No, she's right." Ray said as he climbed the railing and dove off the ship headfirst.

The microwave pinged to let Morty know his leftovers were ready. Grabbing the plate and carrying it to the sitting area, he turned on the TV to kill some time and provide background noise while he ate. *Fortunately, this will all be over tomorrow. I hope.*

Finding a show about world mysteries, he got excited when they started talking about the Dobhar-chú. He knew someone who had traveled around Ireland to track this cryptid. The book wasn't out yet, but he'd heard the stories of his adventures and was excited to learn more about the Otter King.

Ray plummeted downwards. His diving momentum and gravity worked together. He was not much more than a blur to the people on the island heading back to the ship. Those who were a little closer to the gangway saw more clearly and started screaming. Gary wondered what the fuss was about.

Before he had time to look around, or up, Ray landed on his head with all the momentum gravity can give to a 200-pound man flying through the air approaching 80 miles an hour. Both men died instantly on impact.

AFTER HE FINISHED EATING and the show on the Dobhar-chú ended, Morty put his plate in the sink with no intention of cleaning it. *Housekeeping can clean this up tomorrow after I get off the ship.* Walking back to the sitting area, he started watching the next show about mysterious things at a lunatic asylum colloquially called Bedlam Manor. After that, there was going to be a paranormal experience in some haunted jail.

At least I have something fun to watch before I go to bed. With that thought, the phone rang. *Are you kidding me?*

He picked it up to answer. It was Jim.

"What the fuck, Jim? Can't you guys leave me alone? Isn't this incarceration enough for you?" The anger outweighed his common sense when he spoke his mind to his boss.

"Chillax, Morty."

"What do you want?" He said with lingering annoyance but less of a nasty tone to his voice.

"Things are looking up. At least they are a little more favorable now."

Intrigued by a potential change in climate, Morty asked, "How so?"

"Well, now Amanda Resnit's husband, Ray, and the new boss are dead."

"What are you talking about?"

"It appears that Mr. Resnit's grief drove him to suicide. He jumped to his death. Only thing is, he landed on Gary. Both died."

"I guess this is somehow my fault too?" The sarcasm coming from him was palpable.

"Yes. And no, the thing is, neither death was forecasted. Neither was a sanctioned kill or anything like you might expect. So, there will be inquiries."

"Great. So, what now, house arrest after I get out of cabin incarceration?"

"Remember, I told you there was some talk of promoting you? It's increasing. There are a lot more people behind the idea. Your numbers while on vacation are unprecedented."

"Vacation? This hasn't been a damn vacation. This has been a fiasco. No rest for the weary. No rest for the wicked. No rest for the reaper."

"I get that you're angry and things haven't been optimal from your point of view. All I can say is cooperate with anyone who questions you. Heads will roll. Especially in forecasting. But that puts you in a better position. I suspect that before the month comes to a close, you will be given a new position in the organization. One that doesn't require you to reap directly. A permanent paid vacation, if you will."

"A permanent vacation? No reaping? No more people whining for more time, a second chance, or none of that nonsense?

No more racing to meet quotas and reap souls exactly when forecasted?"

"Nope. None of that. Death will get its vacation. Just sit tight and let it happen."

Morty smiled and started thinking about some Mango Jerk Chicken.

About the Author

Brýn Grover writes from the eerie shadows of the Old Dominion where the Bunnyman roams. His short stories blend the weird and the unusual with unsettling horror. As a lifelong fan of B-movies and drive-in nightmares, he channels his passion for the macabre into tales that linger long after the final page.

His collections have included *The Golem and Other Stories*, *All Things End?*, *Jamie's Closet*, and the award-winning *Beyond the Pale*. His upcoming stand-alone book is a cryptid travel adventure entitled *The Otter King: The Search for the Dobhar-Chú*. His writings have also appeared in the anthologies *Dark Corners of the Old Dominion* and *Devour the Rich*.

When not writing, he explores abandoned places, indulges in dark tourism, and pursues his fascination with graveyards and cemeteries as an unapologetic taphophile.

www.ingramcontent.com/pod-product-compliance
Lightning Source LLC
LaVergne TN
LVHW041617070526
838199LV00052B/3185